AF583400

First published 2022, reprinted 2023
Magabala Books Aboriginal Corporation, 1 Bagot Street, Broome, Western Australia
Website: www.magabala.com Email: sales@magabala.com

Magabala Books receives financial assistance from the Commonwealth Government through the Australia Council, its arts advisory body. The State of Western Australia has made an investment in this project through the Department of Local Government, Sport and Cultural Industries. Magabala Books would like to acknowledge the generous support of the Shire of Broome, Western Australia.

Magabala Books is Australia's only independent Aboriginal and Torres Strait Islander publishing house. Magabala Books acknowledges the Traditional Owners of the Country on which we live and work. We recognise the unbroken connection to traditional lands, waters and cultures. Through what we publish, we honour all our Elders, peoples and stories, past, present and future.

Copyright © Sally Morgan, Text 2022
Copyright © Johnny Warrkatja Malibirr, Illustrations 2022

The creators assert their moral rights.

All rights reserved. Apart from any fair dealing for the purposes of private study, research, criticism or review, as permitted under the Copyright Act, no part of this publication may be reproduced by any process whatsoever without the written permission of the publisher.

Designed by Emilia Toia
Printed in China by Everbest Printing Company

ISBN Print 978-1-922613-64-6
ISBN ePDF 978-1-922613-63-9

This title is proudly supported by the ALIA Online Storytime program, through the Australian Government RISE Fund

A catalogue record for this book is available from the National Library of Australia

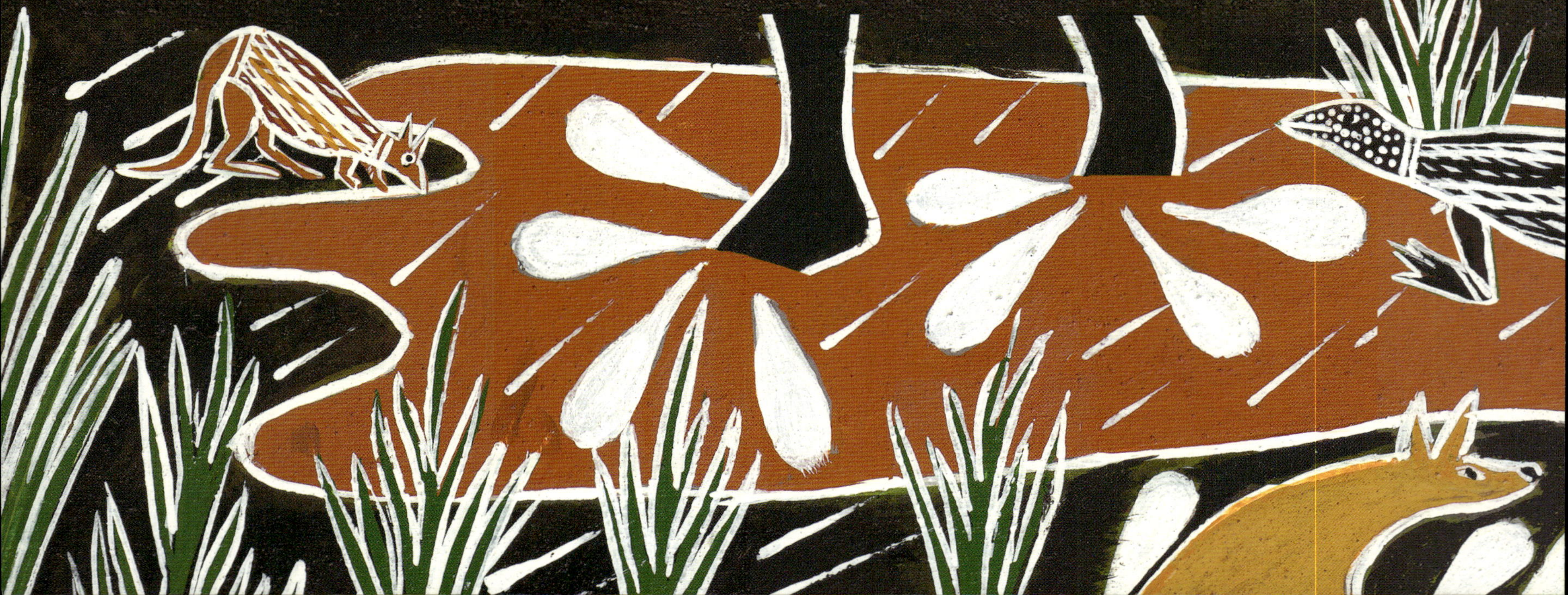

Thank you rain!

Sally Morgan &
Johnny Warrkatja Malibirr

LOOK, the sky is changing

Rain is coming in...

pitter - patter

Raindrops are falling on tree tops.

Birds are
singing
in the rain.

splish -
splosh

Raindrops are wetting dry earth.

Wildflowers
are blooming in
the rain.

drip -
drop
Raindrops
are making
muddy puddles.

Kangaroos are playing in the rain.

plink -
plonk

Raindrops are filling creekbeds.

Animals are drinking in the rain.

LOOK, the sky is changing
A rainbow
is coming in...

I am dancing with
happiness.
Thank you
rain.

Sally Morgan belongs to the Palyku people from the Pilbara, Western Australia. She loves writing stories for children and is excited to once again have such a talented artist as Johnny Warrkatja Malibirr bring her story to life. Sally is the author of the groundbreaking autobiography *My Place.*

Johnny Warrkatja Malibirr is a Yolŋu man from the Ganalbingu clan and is known for his paintings of Ganalbingu song lines as well as his mother's Wägilak clan stories. Along with other members of his clan Johnny keeps culture strong through painting, song, dance and ceremony. He travelled to Canberra in 2000 and performed at the official opening of *Aboriginal Modern Worlds* exhibition at the National Gallery of Australia. Johnny lives in the remote East Arnhem Land community of Gapuwiyak, where he is Chair of the Gapuwiyak Culture and Arts Aboriginal Corporation.

In 2019 Johnny was the winner of Magabala Books' inaugural Kestin Indigenous Illustrator Award, from which he illustrated *Little Bird's Day* the first book he did with author Sally Morgan, followed by *The River. Thank you rain!* is their third book together.

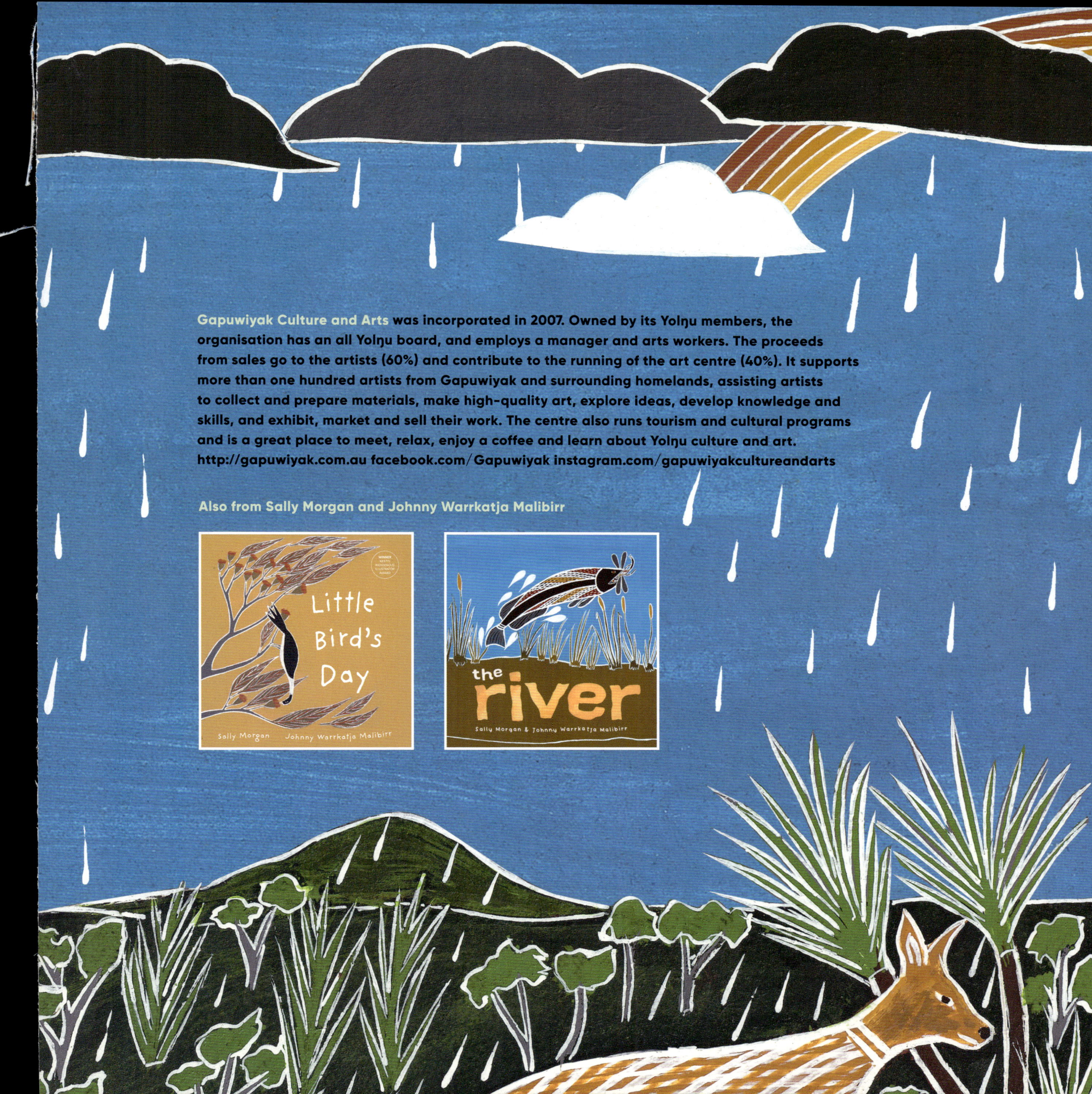

Gapuwiyak Culture and Arts was incorporated in 2007. Owned by its Yolŋu members, the organisation has an all Yolŋu board, and employs a manager and arts workers. The proceeds from sales go to the artists (60%) and contribute to the running of the art centre (40%). It supports more than one hundred artists from Gapuwiyak and surrounding homelands, assisting artists to collect and prepare materials, make high-quality art, explore ideas, develop knowledge and skills, and exhibit, market and sell their work. The centre also runs tourism and cultural programs and is a great place to meet, relax, enjoy a coffee and learn about Yolŋu culture and art. http://gapuwiyak.com.au facebook.com/Gapuwiyak instagram.com/gapuwiyakcultureandarts

Also from Sally Morgan and Johnny Warrkatja Malibirr